Dear Parents:

Congratulations! Your child is taking the first steps on an exciting journey. The destination? Independent reading!

STEP INTO READING® will help your child get there. The program offers five steps to reading success. Each step includes fun stories and colorful art or photographs. In addition to original fiction and books with favorite characters, there are Step into Reading Non-Fiction Readers, Phonics Readers and Boxed Sets, Sticker Readers, and Comic Readers—a complete literacy program with something to interest every child.

Learning to Read, Step by Step!

Ready to Read Preschool–Kindergarten
• big type and easy words • rhyme and rhythm • picture clues
For children who know the alphabet and are eager to begin reading.

Reading with Help Preschool–Grade 1
• basic vocabulary • short sentences • simple stories
For children who recognize familiar words and sound out new words with help.

Reading on Your Own Grades 1–3
• engaging characters • easy-to-follow plots • popular topics
For children who are ready to read on their own.

Reading Paragraphs Grades 2–3
• challenging vocabulary • short paragraphs • exciting stories
For newly independent readers who read simple sentences with confidence.

Ready for Chapters Grades 2–4
• chapters • longer paragraphs • full-color art
For children who want to take the plunge into chapter books but still like colorful pictures.

STEP INTO READING® is designed to give every child a successful reading experience. The grade levels are only guides; children will progress through the steps at their own speed, developing confidence in their reading.

Remember, a lifetime love of reading starts with a single step!

Visit us on the Web!
StepIntoReading.com
rhcbooks.com

Educators and librarians, for a variety of teaching tools, visit us at RHTeachersLibrarians.com

ISBN 978-0-525-64829-1 (trade) — ISBN 978-0-525-64830-7 (lib. bdg.)

Printed in the United States of America

10 9 8 7 6 5 4

nickelodeon

RUSTY RIVETS

TIGERBOT SAVES THE DAY!

adapted by Kristen L. Depken

based on the teleplay
"Frankie's Botasaur" by Susan Kim

illustrated by Donald Cassity

Random House 🏠 New York

Rusty and Ruby
are working outside.

A boy named Frankie
skates over.
He has just moved to town.

Frankie made
his own skateboard.
He says he is
a great inventor!

Frankie thinks
Botasaur is cool.
He wants to make
Botasaur even cooler!

Rusty and Ruby
go inside for a snack.
Frankie sneaks over.

He programs Botasaur to
act like a dino, not a dog.

But he makes a mistake.

Botasaur acts like a big frog!
Botasaur hops away
with Frankie.

Rusty and Ruby

follow in their cars.

Botasaur hops to an island!
Rusty and Ruby
cannot drive on water.

They turn their cars
into boats!

Frankie tries again.

Uh-oh.

He programs Botasaur

to act like a goat!

Botasaur
climbs a mountain.
Rusty and Ruby use
climbing arms to follow.

Frankie programs
Botasaur to act
like a fierce dino!

Roar!

Botasaur's big roar
causes a rockslide.
The rocks push them
off a cliff!

Rusty and Ruby
must help.
They make a plan.

They build
a new robot—Tigerbot!

Tigerbot reaches down
to Frankie and Botasaur.
He saves them!

Rusty fixes

Botasaur's chip.

He is back to normal!

Frankie sees that Botasaur
is fun the way he is.

Tigerbot thinks Botasaur is fun, too!

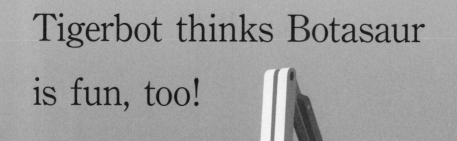

© Spin Master Ltd.

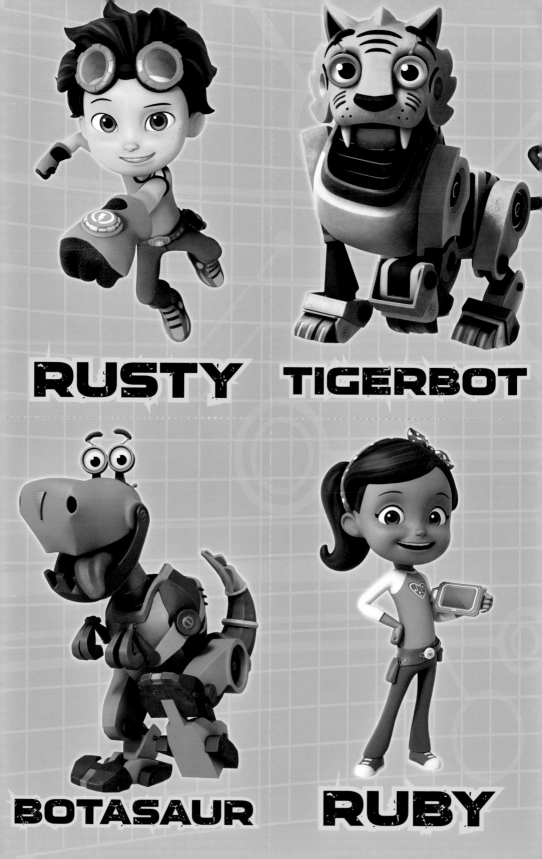

RUSTY

TIGERBOT

BOTASAUR

RUBY

RUBY

BOTASAUR

TIGERBOT

RUSTY